The Snowy Advent

Little Wolf

Written by
Catherine Veitch

Illustrated by
Fabrizio di Baldo

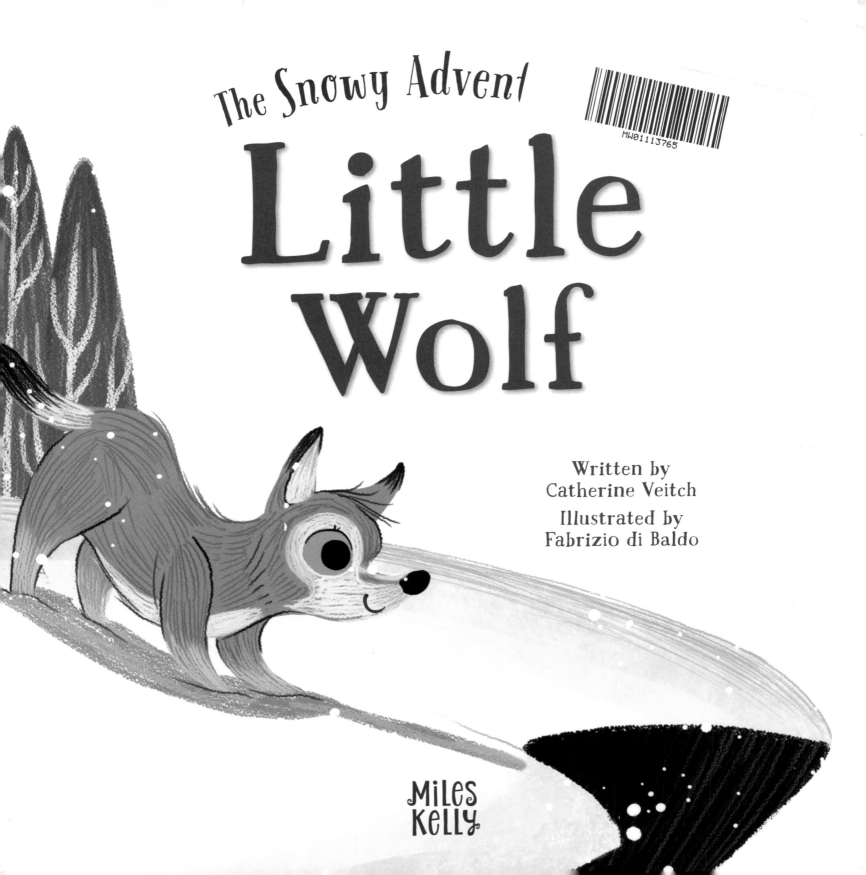

MILES
KELLY

Little Wolf was the smallest grey wolf cub in her pack. She could not wait to grow up and have adventures. The only place she had known since she was born was her den.

However, now they were getting bigger, Little Wolf and her brothers and sisters went outside more.

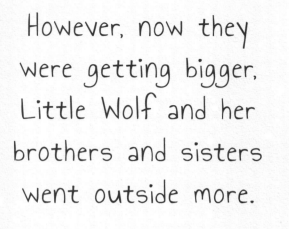

It was winter, and everything in the forest was covered in magical, white snow.

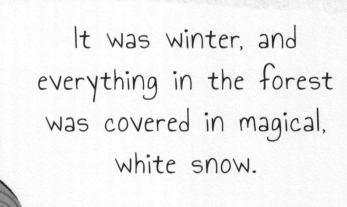

One evening, all of the pack except Little Wolf left to go on a hunt. Even her brothers and sisters went this time.

As the smallest, Little Wolf had to stay behind. But she wanted an adventure and was not going to wait for her pack to return.

I will have an adventure of my own!

Walking in the snow with her large paws was easier than Little Wolf thought. But it was so cold! She was glad she had a thick fur coat to keep her warm. Suddenly, a loud voice called out to Little Wolf.

Crunch!

Hello, little one! My name is Evgeni, I am an elk.

Little Wolf stared at this strange new animal. He looked like he had trees growing out of his head!

"Wolves hunt elks," said Little Wolf, but she wanted to be friends with Evgeni.

"What exciting things do you do in the forest?" asked Little Wolf curiously.

"I find tasty water plants to snack on in the river," replied Evgeni. With that, he stepped into the freezing water and set off swimming.

Little Wolf crouched down, took a deep breath, and was about to jump in when...

"Howwwwwl...
Howwwwwl!"

It was the wolf pack
returning from their hunt.

"Quick, run Evgeni! Or my
pack will eat you!" shouted
Little Wolf.

"Goodbye Little Wolf!"
shouted Evgeni, and
he galloped away.

Little Wolf raced back inside the den just in time. Her pack brought back some fresh meat from their hunt.

Then the pack were off again. Eeew!

"What's that smell?" wondered Little Wolf. She soon found out, as a big, wet, twitching nose poked inside the den, drawn by the fresh meat.

"I hope you don't mind if I help myself to some meat," said a smelly wolverine. He was much bigger than Little Wolf, so she thought it was best not to stop him.

"Ah, that's better," said the wolverine. "I haven't eaten for a few days." The wolverine was called Vasili. Little Wolf bravely asked him what thrilling things he had found in the forest.

"You never know what surprises you will find under the snow," said Vasili, whose super sensitive nose could sniff out anything. "And look, I found this tasty meat, and you!"

Suddenly there came a
Howwwwwwwl!
The wolf pack was
coming back.

"Run Vasili! Or my pack will eat you!"
shouted Little Wolf. She dragged the meat
outside. "If the pack come into the den they
will smell that a stranger has been here."

"There's not much meat left," said Little Wolf's mother. "What a big appetite for such a small wolf!"

Some more meat was left for Little Wolf, then the pack went off to hunt again.

Thanks Mum!

Again Little Wolf was left alone.
Except she did not feel like she was alone.
"Is there anyone there?" she stammered.

"Whooo-ooo-ooo-ooo,
whooo-ooo-ooo-ooo!"

came the reply. The forest was
scary in the evening.

Hello, Little Wolf, I'm Olga, a grey owl.

"Are you going to eat me?" asked Little Wolf, looking at Olga's sharp beak and hooked talons.

"Of course not, you're too big for me to eat," said Olga.

"Do you find the forest an exciting place to live?" asked Little Wolf.

"Yes – I always see amazing animals when I'm soaring over the forest," replied Olga.

She fluffed her feathers and went on, "Tigers, reindeer, red foxes, leopards... we are all so different, but we all share the forest."

Little Wolf felt lucky to live among the creatures who shared the forest.

Later, Little Wolf asked her pack about the wonders of their home.

"The forest is beautiful, but it is also important," said her father. "Did you know it can change the weather?"

The
End